HOOPS

12

44

5

23

HOOPS

For all good sports, whoever and wherever they are
—A.R.

For Phoebe Yeh, with heartfelt thanks
—P.M.

Brendan and Belinda and the Slam Dunk!
Text copyright © 2007 by Anne Rockwell
Illustrations copyright © 2007 by Paul Meisel
Manufactured in China.

For information address HarperCollins Children's Books, a division of HarperCollins Publishers,
1350 Avenue of the Americas, New York, NY 10019.
www.harpercollinschildrens.com

Library of Congress Cataloging-in-Publication Data
Rockwell, Anne F.
Brendan and Belinda and the slam dunk! / by Anne Rockwell ;
illustrated by Paul Meisel.— 1st ed. p. cm.
Summary: Brendan and Belinda and their dad, Mr. Porker, learn that being a
good sport means playing the game well and having fun too.
ISBN-10: 0-06-028443-9 (trade bdg.) ISBN-13: 978-0-06-028443-5 (trade bdg.)
ISBN-10: 0-06-028447-1 (lib. bdg.) ISBN-13: 978-0-06-028447-3 (lib. bdg.)
[1. Basketball—Fiction. 2. Brothers and sisters— Fiction.
3. Sportsmanship—Fiction.] I. Meisel, Paul, ill. II. Title.
PZ7.R5943Br 2007 2003001817 [E]—dc22 CIP AC

Typography by Rachel L. Schoenberg
1 2 3 4 5 6 7 8 9 10
❖
First Edition

By Anne Rockwell
Illustrated by Paul Meisel

HarperCollinsPublishers

23
23

Mr. Porker loved basketball. When he became the father of twins, Brendan and Belinda, he wasted no time teaching them to shoot hoops.

The twins were quick learners. Brendan's first words were "**slam dunk!**" Belinda could dribble a ball as soon as she could walk.

When they were old enough, Mr. Porker signed them up for the All-Hoops Parents and Kids League. The whole family played every Saturday afternoon.

Brendan and Belinda were sensational. All the other parents said so, which made Mr. and Mrs. Porker very proud. The Porker twins always dribbled the ball fast across the court. They never ran with it. They never banged into other players.

They almost always made their shots, and they could play defense, too.

Mr. Porker encouraged the twins to watch games with him on TV, to see how the superstars did it. And just before every game, Mr. Porker would yell out, "Okay, guys! Be like Mike! You can do it! I know you can!"

Brendan and Belinda always dunked.

One day Mr. Porker brought home a big chalkboard. "No TV tonight, guys," he announced. "We're going to work on plays."

"But Dad," wailed Belinda. "Remember? Our favorite TV show, 'Berkshire Brats,' is going to be on in a few minutes."

Mr. Porker said, "Okay, guys. But we have to go over plays as soon as the show's over."

23

5

A few weeks later Mr. Porker came home from work bursting with joy. "Guess what, guys," he said. "We've been invited to join the Jump Shot Juniors! Coach Buttinsky saw you play and figures you're ready for the best team in town."

"But I want to play in All-Hoops with our friends," said Brendan.

"Me too," said Belinda.

"We'll still play with them Saturdays," said Mr. Porker. "But Friday nights we play with the Jump Shot Juniors, and Sunday afternoons we practice with them. Come on—we've got to hurry!"

So Brendan and Belinda put on their jerseys, shorts, and high-tops, and they all drove across town to the Jump Shot Juniors league headquarters.

JUMP SHOT
Juniors

Brendan and Belinda both scored right at the beginning. Mr. Porker was so proud of them that he treated them to ice-cream cones after the game.

“Yes, sir,” he said as he drove home with the big, white moon shining round as a basketball above the houses. “You guys sure do know how to be like Mike.”

But Brendan and Belinda didn’t hear him. They were both sound asleep.

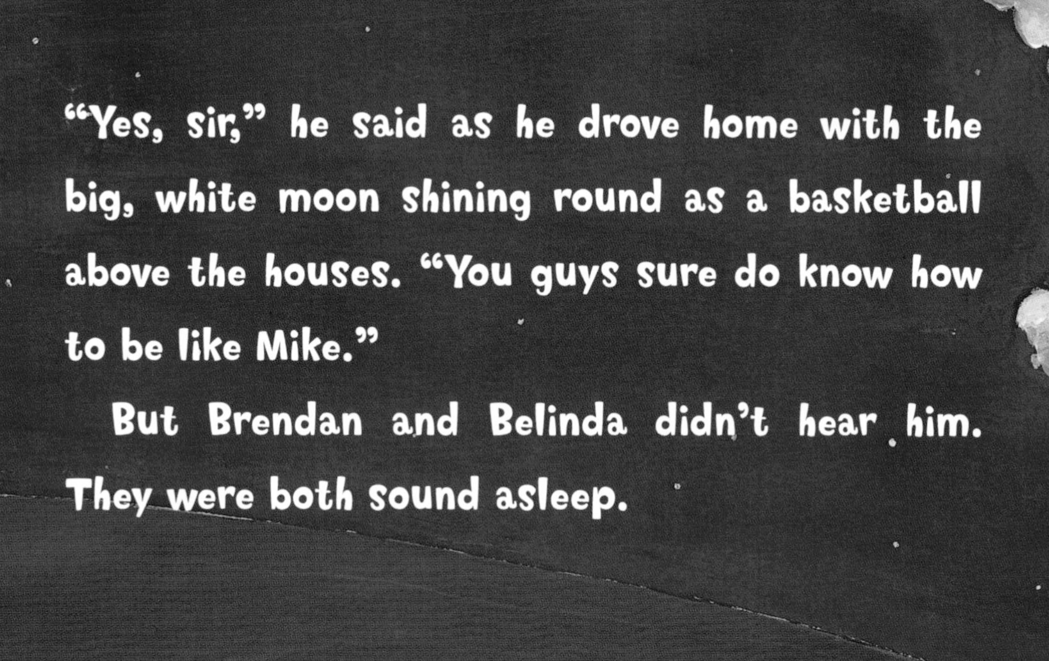

Every Friday night the twins played with the Jump Shot Juniors.

Every Saturday afternoon they played with the All-Hoops Parents and Kids League.

Every Sunday afternoon they practiced with the Jump Shot Juniors.

Every night they reviewed basketball plays with Mr. Porker. It was exhausting.

Late one Saturday night it began to snow. By Sunday morning everything was white.

"Yippee!" yelled Brendan and Belinda. They ran outside and began building a snowman.

Mr. Porker raced after them. "It may take longer to get to the gym with all this snow. We need to leave now."

"We didn't finish our snowman," said the twins.

But Mr. Porker insisted they had to leave.

Morgan Brownbear was making his way up the street in snowshoes. “Are you coming to the park?” he called out to the twins.

They shook their heads. Nina Jane Monkey and her parents were skiing down the hill. Chip O’Hare and Katie Catz were sledding. All their friends were playing in the snow.

Brendan and Belinda began crying. "We don't want to play basketball!" they said. "We want to play in the snow with our friends."

"But you're so good at basketball," said Mr. Porker.

"All we ever do is play basketball. We want to be good at sledding and skiing and snowshoeing too!" cried Belinda.

"Don't you want to be superstars? Don't you want to be like Mike?" Mr. Porker asked sadly.

"Well—maybe we'll be superstars someday," said Brendan, just to cheer him up.

"But not yet?" said Mr. Porker.

"Right," said Belinda. "Not yet."

Mr. Porker sighed as he called Coach Buttinsky on his cell phone to say that Brendan and Belinda were going to take some time out from basketball. And that made Brendan and Belinda very happy.

"You're a good sport, Dad!" they said.

Mrs. Porker saw them putting the sleds and toboggan on top of the car. She said, "Wait for me! I want to go sledding too!"

The Porkers went sledding all afternoon.

When they got home, Brendan and Belinda finished building their snowman, then had hot chocolate with marshmallows on top. As Belinda stirred hers, she said, "Dad, you're a good sport."

"So are you," said Mr. Porker. He gave her and Brendan a high five.

Now, the twins no longer played for the Jump Shot Juniors. But every Saturday afternoon all the Porkers played with the All-Hoops Parents and Kids League.

HOOPS
HOOPS
22
5
29

HOOPS
2
16
HOOPS
HOOPS
32